Fly Away Home

Written and illustrated by
Shoo Rayner

TED SMART

Ladybird is on the tree.

Ladybird is on the leaf.

Ladybird is on the shed.

Ladybird is on the pond.

Ladybird is on the flower.

Ladybird is happy.

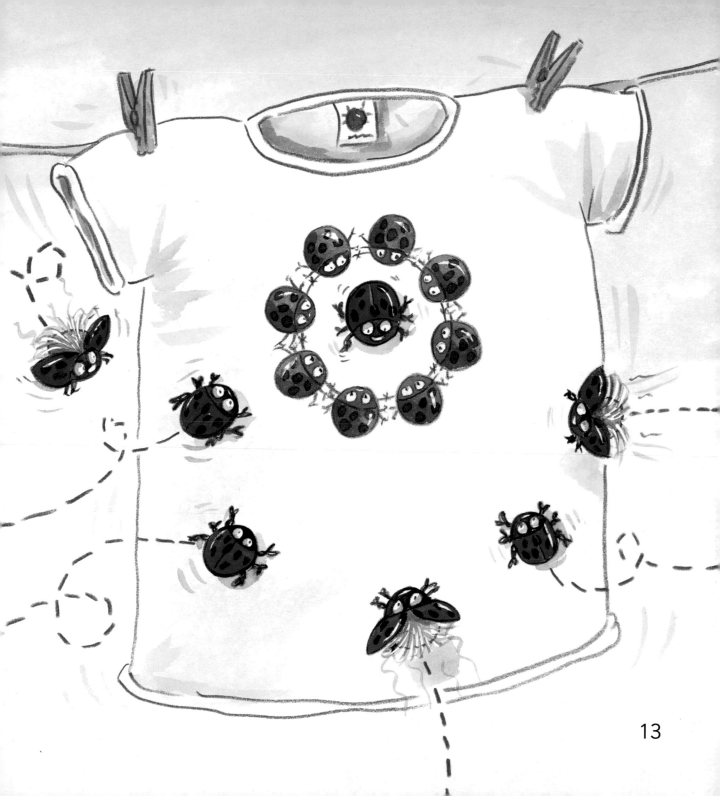

🐾 Ideas for helping your child 🐾

Before you start

- Look at the front cover together. What can you see? How do you think the ladybird feels?

- Read the title. What do you think the book will be about?

Help with reading

- Point to the words as you read, to reinforce that we read from left to right. Explain that these words make up the story and tell you what to say.

- Introduce the phrase 'Ladybird is on the...' and encourage your child to repeat the phrase with you.

- Ask your child what they can see on the left-hand page. Where does the ladybird land? Point to the pictures of new words: tree, leaf, shed, etc.

- Encourage your child to sound out the first letters of each new word to help them identify it. Praise them every time they get a word right.

- On the right-hand page, match the detail of the picture to the picture on the left. Look at the expressions of the creatures. What does your child think they might feel or say?

Help with discussion

- The story is based on fitting in. Talk with your child about the ladybird and other insects and how they feel. Why does the ladybird not fit in each time? And why does the ladybird finally feel happy? Has your child ever felt like the ladybird?

- Finally, talk about the last double-page of the book. Can your child follow the path of the ladybird and correctly remember the names of the places where the ladybird went? Can they remember the order in which they came in the story?

Taking it further

- Look in the park or garden and see if you can find any of the creatures from the story.